7.95

E   Politi, Leo
c.8   DEC 19   Mr. Fong's toy
       shop   Y   8 3 0

JUN   2 1982   *Lois Arng*
OCT   4 1982   *Ellen Tice*
DEC   6 1982   *M. Leiser*
      1982   *D. Wells*

E   Politi, Leo
c.8   Mr. Fong's toy shop.   Scribner's,
      c1978.
        [26] p.

      I. Title

7.95   LC 78-1547

Mr. Fong's Toy Shop

Mr. Fong's Toy Shop

by

Leo Politi

CHARLES SCRIBNER'S SONS

Copyright © 1978 Leo Politi

Library of Congress Cataloging in Publication Data
Politi, Leo, 1908-
Mr. Fong's toy shop.
SUMMARY: A toymaker and his young friends prepare a
shadow puppet play for the Moon Festival in Chinatown in
Los Angeles.
[1. Chinese Americans—Fiction. 2. Puppets and
puppet-plays—Fiction] I. Title.
PZ7.P753Mr   [E]   78-1547
ISBN 0-684-15583-4

1 3 5 7 9 11 13 15 17 19 MD/C 20 18 16 14 12 10 8 6 4 2

Printed in the United States of America

Mr. Fong makes and sells toys in a small shop in Chinatown in Los Angeles. He likes to make toys like the ones he played with as a boy in the little mountain village in China where he was born. While he works he enjoys remembering those early days.

Mr. Fong's friends include many children. The children of the nearby shopkeepers visit him almost every day. Sometimes they come to buy his toys. And sometimes they come just to watch him work and listen to his stories.

"Good morning, Mr. Fong," they say as they enter one by one.

"Good morning, Jade. Good morning, Sam. Good morning, Niu. Good morning, Mei-lau. Good morning, Lily. Good morning, Jeff. Good morning, Kristal. Good morning, Chen," Mr. Fong replies.

One day he showed the children how to make magic sticks out of a plain bamboo branch. Then he showed them how to juggle the sticks just as the jugglers used to do in the market place of his boyhood village.

Another day, as he carved a yo-yo out of a scrap of wood, he told the children how the toy had originated in China and how, long ago, in the rich courts there, the reels were made of gold, silver, or ivory studded with jewels.

"Some believe that if you spin it fast enough, the yo-yo produces a whistle that will expel evil spirits," Mr. Fong said. Later he let the children play with the toys and soon his shop was buzzing with young jugglers juggling magic sticks and spinning yo-yos.

The time of the Moon Festival was near and many preparations were necessary. The Moon Festival comes in mid-autumn when the moon is at its brightest and fullest, and the harvest has been gathered. In China it is the time when friends and families meet to celebrate the Moon Goddess, Chang-O. They gaze at the moon in wonderment and write poems about the beauty of the moon and the night.

Mr. Fong told the children the legend of Chang-O, the Moon Goddess, who lives in a palace in the moon with her helper, a white hare.

Chang-O was the lovely wife of a powerful king who reigned in China many years ago. The people found a magic seed which would have kept him alive forever. But Chang-O knew her husband to be a tyrant, and not wishing her people to have a cruel king forever, she stole the magic seed and swallowed it herself. As she ate the seed, she rose and went straight up into the moon where she lives to this day. The people were very grateful that lovely Chang-O had saved them from having a wicked king forever, and so every year since they remember her with the Moon Festival.

In Chinatown in Los Angeles, the children celebrate this occasion with a Lantern Parade, and perform songs and dances on an outdoor stage in a neighborhood park.

This year Mr. Fong wanted to prepare a surprise for the people at the Moon Festival. He wanted to produce a shadow puppet play on the stage in the park to honor Chang-O, and he told the children that each of them could take part. The children were very pleased and excited by the idea and were eager to start.

As they watched, Mr. Fong showed them how a shadow puppet is made. First he drew the figures of animals and people on cardboard, and then he cut them out. Next, he fastened these to sticks which would be used to hold the figures and make them move. Finally he stretched a sheet over a wooden frame and placed it on his large work table as a screen.

Before he began to perform, Mr. Fong darkened the room except for a very bright light above and behind the small stage so that when the puppets were held and moved close to the screen their shadows would be projected on it. Then, moving the figures quickly and speaking the lines, Mr. Fong showed the children how a shadow puppet show is performed.

The old man created a skit between a crow and a tiger—two of the puppets the children had watched him make. The tiger wanted to catch the crow, but every time he tried, the bird flew away. This made the crow very angry and he dived on the tiger's tail and bit it!

The tiger went through so many contortions to catch the bird that the children laughed and laughed. The tiger finally got so tired that he flopped down and fell asleep.

Soon the children took turns making the puppets
perform. Mei-lau made a puppet dance, Jeff made the

boy ride a tiger, and then they all made the puppets
do exciting things. The puppets seemed to come alive.

The next day Mr. Fong showed his friends some old Chinese puppets. He lifted them carefully from a shelf and arranged them on the screen so the children could observe all of the fine detail. There was a dragon, a phoenix, a brave soldier on horseback, and a beautiful princess riding over a bridge into the forest. The children thought the puppets were very beautiful. Mr. Fong told them that shadow puppets originally came from China, and that they were made from dried animal skin because it was found to be very durable and transparent.

Then Mr. Fong asked the children if they wanted to hear his favorite legend about how the shadow puppets originated.

"Yes!" they cried as they closely gathered around the old man.

"In ancient China," Mr. Fong began, "there lived an Emperor who became very angry with his two court jesters. He ordered them to leave and never return. When his anger subsided, he found life dull without them. So he ordered his Minister to search for the two jesters and not to return until he found them. The Minister searched and searched but to no avail. As he was about to give up all hope, he met a fisherman carrying two huge fish. Suddenly it occurred to him to take the skin of the fish, dry them, and cut out two figures that looked like the two jesters.

"When the Minister returned to court he made the figures perform behind a lighted curtain. They looked so real and he had mimicked their voices so well that the Emperor found he was even more pleased with the shadow jesters than with the real ones.

"From then on," Mr. Fong told his young friends, "shadow puppet plays became very popular and were performed in every city and village in China."

During the following days the children made puppets, moved them about, and learned their lines for the play. They worked very hard because they wanted to give their best performance and make Mr. Fong proud of them.

On the day of the festival, children came from everywhere carrying colorful lanterns they had made for the special occasion. They came dressed in the dainty Chinese clothes that they always wore for festive events.

In the little park where the festival was taking place, many lovely booths had been set up in which foods and soft drinks were sold. In one booth sweets shaped like butterflies and cooked in deep fat attracted the children who lined up to buy them. Another favorite was the moon cake. Moon cakes are so good that they are given as gifts during the festival. The giving of moon cakes as gifts celebrated the time during the Yuan Dynasty when the Mongol oppressors were defeated by the Chinese who rallied their forces with secret messages concealed in the moon cakes presented by one family to another.

When evening came and the full moon rose in the sky, the children gathered for the Lantern Parade. The lanterns were very beautiful and fancy and of every shape imaginable. Jade carried a lantern in the shape of a large lotus flower, Sam's lantern was shaped like an airplane, Kristal's like a pheasant, Chen's a toy horse, Lily's like the white hare that lives in the moon, Mei-lau's in the shape of the moon with the lovely goddess Chang-O painted on it. Jeff came with the huge fish lantern from Mr. Fong's toy shop.

The parade began in the midst of bursting firecrackers and the loud beating of the drums and gongs. The swift and lively lion and dragon dancers led the procession. It was a beautiful parade. The children with lanterns looked like a trail of hundreds of fireflies gleaming in the dark. They chanted the Moonlight Songs on the way.

People everywhere were moved by the beauty of it and applauded as the procession went by. Mr. Fong was very proud of the children.

Moonlight Song

月 光 曲

When the parade ended, the children returned to the platform in the park where the stage show was about to begin.

First, four little girls did the Ribbon Dance. They danced with huge ribbons, making them float gracefully in the air to dramatize the movements of the clouds and the ocean waves, and the graceful motions of the dragon floating in the air.

Clowns and acrobats then performed. And Jeff performed with the yo-yo. He spun it so fast that it whistled. Sam juggled the magic sticks, without dropping one! Everyone applauded.

At last the big moment arrived for Mr. Fong and the children to begin the shadow puppet play.

Mr. Fong narrates and explains the stage setting of the little village in China where he grew up. He mimics the voices of people coming and going along the busy mule trail to the village.

In the next scene of the play there are sounds of gaiety and laughter as children play in the village courtyard. Brightly colored kites soar high in the clouds. Children walk and sway on stilts made of bamboo poles, and do somersaults as if they are on a trapeze.

As the drummer plays louder and faster, a boy comes dashing across the stage with a ferocious dragon mask over his face. He crawls around and growls to frighten the playing children. The sounds of laughter and general excitement grow louder.

In the next scene night has come to the village and the children are in their homes sound asleep on floor mats. But wait! Something strange is about to happen. In the silence and darkness of the night appears a mysterious silhouetted figure that prowls around and steals the children's toys.

The children are very sad when they awake in the morning to find their toys gone. There is little the villagers can do to apprehend the thief, but one night when the thief is on the prowl again, a full moon suddenly appears from behind the mountains and shines brighter than ever before.

The thief panics and runs, but everywhere he runs there is the bright light from the moon and no place for him to hide. In shame he is captured by the villagers. The thief returns all the stolen toys and promises not to steal again.

Thanks to Chang-O, the kind and beautiful Moon Goddess, the children are happy again and the villagers live in peace ever after.

Mr. Fong was very proud of the children's performance. He told them they were good enough now to make puppet plays of their own.

As Mr. Fong went home that night, the bright moon lighted his way. On the park grounds he found a piece of paper. He picked it up. On it was one of the many poems the children had written:

Holding hands we play tonight,
In this starry moonlit night,
All around us a silver glow,
Thanks to lovely Chang-O.

As we gaze at the moon,
Many Ahs! Ohs! and Uhs!
And we see a white hare,
Smiling, leaping through the air.

When came the silence of the gong,
All said, thank you, Mr. Fong,
For being to us so nice,
We all wish you a good night.

Mr. Fong smiled, and as he folded the paper and put it in his pocket he made up a little poem of his own:

Good night, children dear,
Until tomorrow will appear,
Then I hope to see you all,
Back playing in my store.